FOR MAGGIE PHILBRICK

MIRA CATALINA
PALOS VERDES PENINSULA UNIFIED SCHOOL DISTRICT

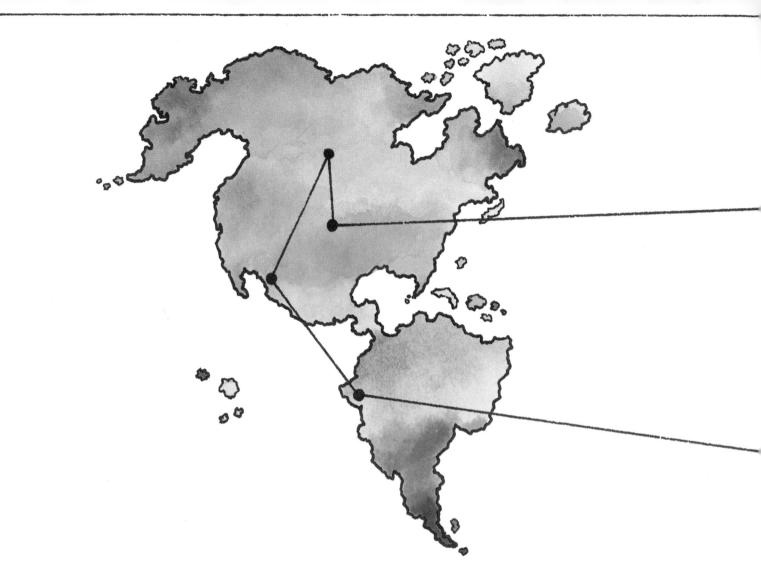

Clarion Books/a Houghton Mifflin Company imprint/52 Vanderbilt Avenue, New York, NY 10017. Text and Illustrations copyright © 1989 by Dick Gackenbach. All rights reserved. For information about permission to reproduce selections from this book, write to Permissions, Houghton Mifflin Company, 2 Park Street, Boston, MA 02108. Printed in the USA. Library of Congress Cataloging-in-Publication Data. Gackenbach, Dick. With love from Gran / Dick Gackenbach. p.   cm.   Summary: A little boy's grandmother decides to see the world, and sends him a present from each place she visits. ISBN 0-89919-842-2   [1. Grandmothers— Fiction.   2. Voyages and travels—Fiction.]   I. Title.   PZ7.G117Wi 1989 cc ng
[E]—dc19   88-35248   CIP
AC

H 10 9 8 7 6 5 4 3 2 1

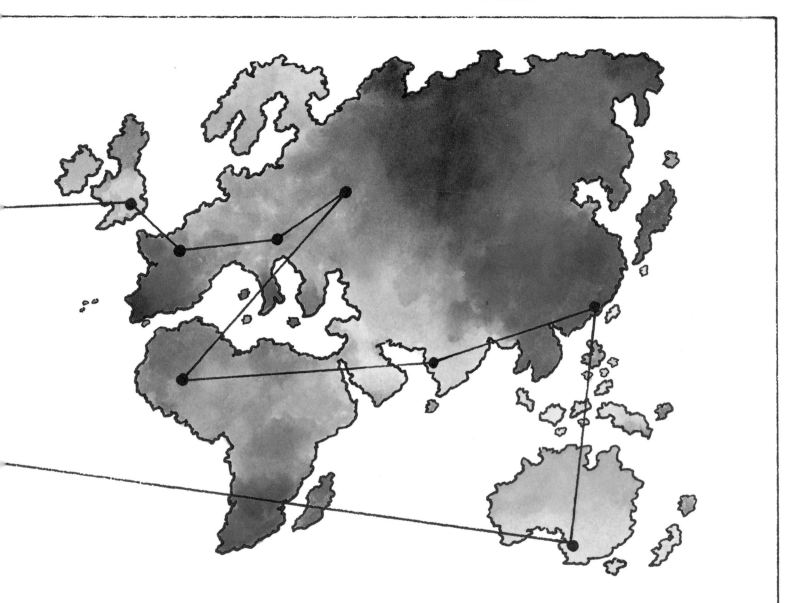

WITH LOVE FROM GRAN

by Dick Gackenbach

CLARION BOOKS
New York

My gran is great.
Her lap fits me just fine.
She makes me homemade jam
sandwiches, and we sit and
shell peas together.
One day she told me,
"I want to see the world before
I get too old."

And off she went—by taxi,

by plane,

by ship,

and by train.

From LONDON,
Gran sent me a castle and crown.

From PARIS came a gold monkey that plays the banjo.

From BUDAPEST,
Gran sent me a gypsy wagon.

From MOSCOW,
a Cossack suit and a beard.

And from TIMBUKTU in Mali,
I got an African mask
and dancing bells for my ankles.

An ivory elephant with ruby eyes
came from BOMBAY.

From HONG KONG, a dragon arrived.

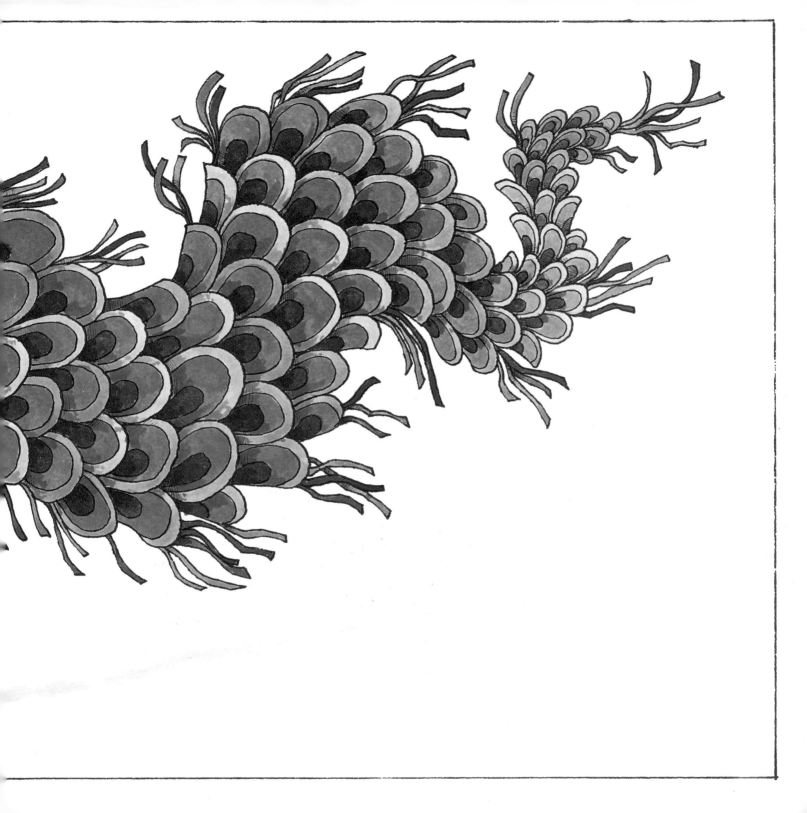

From ADELAIDE, a kangaroo.

From LIMA, a llama.

And guess what from CHIHUAHUA?
A little Chihuahua!

From **SASKATCHEWAN**, in Canada,
I got a telegram.
"I'll be home tomorrow," it read.
"Love from Gran."

That was the best present
of all...
when Gran came
home.

I still fit on her lap,
and we still shell peas together.